Pictures

presents

HOMEWARD BOUND II

Lost in San Francisco

WALT DISNEP Pictures

presents

HOMEWARD BOUND II

Lost in San Francisco

A novel by Nancy Krulik
Based on the motion picture from Walt Disney Pictures
Based upon characters from *The Incredible Journey*
by Sheila Burnford
Story by Julie Hickson and Chris Hauty
Screenplay by Chris Hauty
Produced by Barry Jossen
Directed by David R. Ellis

Walt Disney Pictures
presents

HOMEWARD BOUND II

Lost in San Francisco

Chapter 1

"Steady now . . . steady . . ."

Chance, planning his attack, eyed his prey. He circled the winged creature for a while. Then, in a split second, the black-and-white dog flexed his muscles, opened his huge mouth, and lunged. "You . . . are . . . history!" he barked.

But Chance wasn't fast enough. The quick, wild . . . butterfly flew off into the sky, leaving Chance with a mouth full of dandelion seeds.

Still, Chance wasn't too disappointed. After all, he didn't *need* to eat the butterfly. He got plenty of food from his family, the Seavers. Chance had started out as a poor orphan in a dog pound. But that all changed the day little Jamie Seaver walked in and chose Chance to be his dog.

Chance wasn't the only pet in the Seaver household. There was also Shadow, an old, wise golden retriever who belonged to Jamie's big brother, Peter. Shadow was a kind dog, and he made it his business to take care of Chance.

As far as Chance was concerned, two dogs in the house would have been just fine. Unfortunately, he also had to share the place with Sassy, a fluffy Himalayan cat who belonged to Jamie's sister, Hope. Sassy really liked picking on Chance. And Chance really liked teasing Sassy.

All in all, life at the Seavers' was pretty good for Chance—three square meals a day, plenty of room to roam, and not bad company, as far as humans go. Still, sometimes, Chance longed for something more. A little adventure. But until an adventure came around, Chance was happy playing with Jamie.

At least he used to be. These days, Jamie didn't seem to notice Chance. All Jamie wanted to do was play some game called baseball.

Chance wandered into the house and planted himself outside Jamie's door. He saw Jamie look under his bed for something. Chance figured Jamie was searching for him.

"Yo! Jamie! Over here! I'm *waitinnnggg!*" Chance barked. Jamie, of course, didn't know what Chance was saying, but Chance's barking usually got the message across.

Chance watched as Jamie moved a bureau away from the wall. A baseball slid off the top of the bureau and rolled, stopping just in front of Chance.

"All right!" Chance whooped, snatching the baseball in his teeth. "Fetch, it is!"

Jamie turned to look at Chance. Chance wagged his stubby little tail with delight.

"NO! NOT MY BARRY BONDS AUTOGRAPHED BASEBALL!" Jamie shouted, stealing the ball from Chance's grip. Already more than a little bit upset about having to miss some baseball games to go on a family camping trip, Jamie wasn't about to let Chance chew up one of his most prized possessions.

Chance watched in horror as Jamie raced back

into his room and slammed the door, right in the dog's face. Chance couldn't believe it! "What a grouch!" the dog mumbled as he trotted through the hallway and down the stairs. "Could have been a sudden gust of wind," Chance reasoned. "Or maybe his hand slipped. Sure, that's it. He didn't really mean to slam the door in my face. I'll forgive him . . . this time."

With Jamie holed up in his room, Chance needed to find something else to do. Bothering Sassy seemed like a fun idea. Chance picked up her scent coming from the foyer.

"I thought I smelled litter box," he said. (Unlike humans, animals can understand one another's languages, perfectly.)

"Why? Why couldn't I have been adopted by a family with cats?" Sassy complained.

Chance ignored her. "Come on, feline. You know the routine: I chase you. You run up a tree. I bark like crazy."

That was not Sassy's idea of fun. "Scram, rubber-face," she spat at him. "Go find yourself a squirrel."

Chance nudged Sassy with his big black snout. The beautiful cat rose to her feet, sighed, and ran up the stairs. Unfortunately, at exactly the same time, Mrs. Seaver was on her way *down* the stairs, carrying clothing, luggage, and camping gear. Sassy's sudden movement startled Mrs. Seaver. She dropped everything!

"AVALANCHE!" Chance yelled as the pile of tents, canteens, shorts, sunscreen, and bug spray came flying down the stairs. A pair of boxer shorts landed on Chance's head. "Hey! Who turned out the lights?" he shouted as he tried to shake the underpants from his face.

Sassy had a good laugh at the ridiculous sight. "As a fashion statement," she remarked, "this ranks right up there with the time you got the marble stuck up your nose."

"You'll get yours, flea mat," Chance retorted with a growl.

Shadow padded into the foyer. "Stop it, Chance," the old dog advised. "You're not helping anything."

"Go ahead, Mr. Dog of the Year. Stick up for our human oppressors," Chance teased. Then he stopped and thought about what Shadow had just said. "Not helping what?" he asked.

Shadow stood proudly. "They're leaving home again. Only this time . . . they're taking us with them."

Chapter 2

Chance breathed a sigh of relief. The Seavers were taking him with them. Good thing. Chance did not want to relive last year's vacation. Back then, the Seavers had gone on a trip, leaving Chance, Shadow, and Sassy on a ranch that belonged to a friend of Mrs. Seaver's. But the Seavers didn't come back for what seemed like a very long time. Shadow said he knew it wasn't like Peter to abandon him. Something had to be wrong!

So Shadow, Sassy, and Chance had set out for home on their own. The Seaver house was very far away from the ranch—across miles and miles of mountains. Along the way, Sassy almost drowned, Shadow fell in a ditch and injured his leg, and Chance got stuck with porcupine quills. Still, they'd made it. The three of them, working together, had made it all the way home.

Chance did not want to go through that again. Adventure was one thing. That trip had been quite another.

* *

Chance's ears perked up as he heard Jamie's footsteps pounding down the stairs. "Back in five minutes!" Jamie shouted. "Bye!"

Chance skipped off after his boy. "All right! Outdoor duty!" he yelped.

"No, Chance, you stay!" Jamie called back to him. "Stay home!"

"Home?" Chance whimpered. "Home is safe. Home is boring." No way Chance was staying home while Jamie had all the fun. Jamie was probably only kidding anyway, Chance reasoned. "Jamie, my man, wait for me!" he called out.

Chance had no idea where Jamie was heading until they reached the baseball diamond. "Oh no! Not baseball!" Chance mumbled. "I thought we

7

were going to have some fun!" Chance hated baseball. Baseball was something Jamie did without him.

Crash! A line drive flew right past first base.

Looks just like a rabbit, Chance thought as the white ball flew by. Quick as a wink, he took off after the ball, snagging it in his teeth.

Jamie ran to Chance. *All right! A game of fetch!* Chance thought.

No such luck. Jamie snatched the ball from the dog's teeth. "How many times do I have to tell you—stay off the field!"

A heavyset boy walked over to Jamie. "Get the dog outta here, Seaver!" he yelled.

Chance glared at the fat boy. *Nobody yells at Jamie!* Chance leaped toward the boy's leg and jawed down on his baseball glove. "Give it up, barrel butt!" Chance snarled as he wrestled the glove from the boy.

It took a while for Jamie to convince Chance to give back the glove. Afterward, on the way home, Jamie was really mad. He even called Chance a stupid dog!

Jamie wasn't the only one who was mad. Mr. and Mrs. Seaver were plenty mad, too. But they were mad at Jamie. They'd been looking all over for him. If the Seavers didn't leave right away, they would miss their flight to Maine. Everyone else was already in the car.

Peter got out and took Chance by the collar. He opened the front of a pet carrier and stuffed the dog inside.

"Wait a minute! What did I do?" Chance howled. "Don't you at least have to read me my rights? Somebody call a lawyer!"

"Don't forget to give him his tranquilizer, Peter," Mr. Seaver called from the front seat. Peter nodded and placed a green pill under Chance's tongue. Then Peter closed the back door of the station wagon and took his seat next to his brother.

Chance started to panic. He was certain Jamie was sending him back to the pound. "Jamie! Help!" he cried out. "Whatever I did, I didn't mean it. Don't take me back to the pound!"

Chance peered out through a small vent hole in his pet carrier. "Somebody ought to stick *them* in a box. See how they like it," he complained.

Sassy was getting nervous. "Shadow, I don't like this," she said. "They're going to lose us again."

Shadow kept his voice calm. "It's going to be okay, Sassy," he assured her. "Peter promised they wouldn't leave us behind this time."

But Chance wasn't so sure. "Oh yeah? Then explain the little green kibbles they just jammed down our throats."

Shadow thought about that. "You're right, Chance. Those things make me sleepy. Better get rid of it."

"Get rid of it?" Sassy asked. "How? I swallowed mine already."

"You call yourself a cat?" Chance taunted. "All ya gotta do is eat some fur and . . . voilà! An empty stomach." Chance looked down at the pile of vomit by his feet. There lay the tranquilizer, as well as a nickel, a pearl earring, and a little rubber ball.

"Hey! I've been looking for that!" Chance said when he saw the ball.

Shadow and Sassy followed Chance's lead. Now the animals could relax. They were wide awake and able to keep an eye on their humans. The Seaver pets wouldn't be left behind again.

Chapter 3

San Francisco Airport was busy with people going on summer vacations. Peter pulled Shadow's carrier to a large window. "Look, boy!" he exclaimed. "That's the plane we're going to fly to Maine. Know what I mean, old fella? Fly?" Peter raised his arms like wings.

"I see the plane, Peter," Shadow barked. "I understand."

Before they knew it, the animals were placed on a cart with wheels. It was time for them to be loaded into the cargo area of the plane. Peter said good-bye to Shadow. Hope said good-bye to

Sassy. Jamie just scowled. He was mad about missing his baseball games while the family was on vacation.

Sassy, Shadow, and Chance sat quietly as their cases were wheeled outside onto the airfield and loaded onto an airport tractor. The tractor drove them across the airfield toward the plane. Along the way, they saw animals being removed from another plane. The animals had also been given tranquilizers. But unlike the Seaver pets, *those* animals had swallowed them. So the other animals appeared still, quiet, and sluggish.

Chance was frightened. He didn't understand that the animals looked that way because of the tranquilizers. He thought something awful had happened to them on the plane. "Did you see that? Those guys aren't looking so good!"

Sassy used her paws to cover her sensitive ears. The roar of the plane was making her crazy! "My ears! Somebody shut off that horrible noise!"

"Quiet, you two. Everything is going to be okay." Once again, Shadow tried to reassure the others.

Just then, four maintenance workers dressed in jumpsuits with protective hoods passed by. Chance had seen people dressed like that before. Mean people. Dogcatcher people!

"I've seen humans like that before," Chance shouted to Shadow and Sassy. "THEY'RE TAK-ING US TO THE POUND!"

"Chance! Stop it!" Shadow warned.

"*You* stop it, buster! I was born in the bad place. I know what it's like!"

Chance had to escape! He threw all of his weight against the carrier door. Nothing happened. Panic-stricken, Chance rocked back and forth with all of his might. The carrier slipped from the tractor and fell to the floor, splitting into three big pieces. Chance was free!

"Chance!" Shadow yelled out. But it was too late. Chance raced off in the direction of the airline terminal, where he had last seen Jamie. Jamie wouldn't let them take him to the pound!

"Shadow! He's running away," Sassy cried.

Shadow nodded. "We've got to stop him. Can you reach the latch, Sassy?"

"Are you kidding? I can reach it, unhook it, and slap it around for good measure." With that, the resourceful cat used her claws to open the latch on her carrier. The door popped open and Sassy gracefully stepped out. She leaped on top of Shadow's carrier and opened the latch. That wire door sprung open as well. Together, Shadow and Sassy hopped off the tractor and bounded back toward the terminal to find Chance.

Just then, a nearby baggage handler on his coffee break paused to look up from his newspaper and saw a black-and-white dog sprinting toward the terminal. He rubbed his eyes—convinced he was hallucinating—and slowly reopened them to a golden retriever and a Himalayan cat streaking past. Startled, he upended his coffee, soaking his shirt.

But the animals were too preoccupied to notice.

Sassy and Shadow eventually caught up with Chance near the oversize-luggage conveyor belt.

"What's gotten into you, pup?" Shadow asked excitedly between breaths. "We're supposed to be on that plane!"

But Chance did not believe him. "No! Jamie wouldn't abandon me! Not here! Not like this! I'M COMING, LITTLE BUDDY!" he called out, leaping onto the moving belt.

"Come on, Sassy," Shadow called out. "We haven't got much time." The golden retriever leaped onto the conveyor belt. Sassy followed close behind.

Chance stood inside the airport, looking around for Jamie. But Jamie was already on board. When he saw Shadow and Sassy approaching, Chance looked down at the ground, ashamed. "Anybody see a little boy looking for his lost dog?" he asked sheepishly.

Shadow could hold his tongue no longer. "You fool! They're going to leave without us!"

"Not again!" Sassy hissed.

"Yes, again!" Shadow replied. He glared at Chance. "Only this time it's *our* fault!"

Chance flattened his ears and whimpered. *Not* our *fault*, he thought. My *fault*.

C h a p t e r 4

By now, most of the airport ground crew was searching for Chance, Shadow, and Sassy. They wanted to catch them and hold onto them until the Seavers could come and get them. The Seavers had already boarded the plane to Maine. They were buckling themselves in and listening to the flight attendant tell them about oxygen masks, emergency exits, and other airplane safety features. They had no idea that at that very moment their pets were running wildly through San Francisco Airport.

Chance leaped off the baggage carrier and started running toward an exit. Before he knew it, someone jumped on his back and wrestled him to the ground.

"Urghmp miyt sgricllic!" Chance tried to yelp for help, but the airline worker was choking him.

"I've got one! I've got one!" the man cried out.

Shadow let out a deep, frustrated sigh. Once again it was up to him to save the pup. The old retriever jumped forward and barked at the airline worker. He raised his lip and snarled. The startled man took one look at Shadow's sharp teeth and released his grip on Chance.

The animals raced out the door and onto the airfield. Maybe there was still time to catch that plane and get to Maine with the Seavers!

There were a lot of airplanes lined up along the runway for takeoff. "Shadow, which plane is it?" Sassy asked between gasps for air.

Shadow stopped for a moment and looked around. Then he spotted the plane Peter had shown him earlier. It was the first in line.

"There! That's the one," he said, pointing with his front paw.

The giant airliner hurtled toward them, picking up speed as it moved.

"Aren't they going to stop?" Sassy asked Shadow.

"Only if they hit us," Chance barked in fear. "DUCK!"

Sassy, Shadow, and Chance flattened themselves against the warm concrete. The plane raced nearer and nearer toward them and then, suddenly, miraculously, lifted its wheels off the ground and took off into the air.

Chance was afraid to look. Finally the roar of the plane disappeared into the distance. He glanced over at Sassy and smiled. "I didn't die and go to doggie heaven," he teased. "You're still here."

Sassy hissed. "Um, Chance, does my nose detect that certain . . . smell of fear?"

Chance looked down at the puddle between his legs. Whoops! He'd been really scared!

While Chance and Sassy argued, Shadow looked sadly up at the sky. "Good-bye, Peter," he called mournfully.

"I can't believe this has happened again," Sassy said. She stared angrily at Chance.

Chance started to answer but stopped. Better to keep moving than to keep fighting. Already the humans were on their way. Sirens blared from all directions as emergency vehicles chased after the three pets.

There was no way Chance was going to let them catch him. He darted off in the direction of a far-off fence. Shadow and Sassy followed close behind.

As soon as the animals reached the fence, Shadow twisted and turned until he made his way under the fence to freedom. Sassy slipped under in one quick, graceful motion. Chance tried to copy Sassy. But Chance was no graceful cat. He was a big, klutzy dog! Chance's collar got stuck on the fence. He pulled and pulled, but that darn fence would not let go.

"Why . . . does . . . this . . . always . . . happen . . . to ME!" he yelled out.

Chance could sense the airport workers approaching. He had to get free! Those guys were not taking him back to the pound. Not if he could help it, anyway! With one final, mighty push, Chance broke free of his collar and shimmied under the fence.

The three pets raced away to freedom and into the unknown.

Chapter 5

The animals didn't stop running until they reached an open field where they felt safe enough to stop and catch their breath.

"If it weren't for you, I'd be on a plane right now, with Hope," Sassy scolded Chance.

Chance would take criticism like that from Shadow. But he wasn't going to take it from a cat! "If it weren't for me, you'd be a furry pancake of cat guts," Chance shot back.

Sassy sighed. "Why couldn't Jamie have adopted a nice, respectful *cat*?"

Shadow stepped in and stopped the argument.

"*Enough*, Sassy. Chance is part of our family, and that's forever."

Chance's ears flopped down to the sides of his head. "I wouldn't go that far," he remarked wistfully.

"Jamie loves you, Chance, no matter what you think," Shadow assured him. "Now come on, you two. We'd better get going. I want to be home for Peter when he returns."

Sassy looked across the field. There was nothing there but a big dirt hill and an empty stretch of land. "But . . . but which way do we go?" she asked nervously.

Shadow held his regal head high. He sniffed the air a bit and looked around. "I know the way," he said finally. "I can *feel* it." Shadow motioned over the hill with his snout and started climbing.

"Yo, Coach," Chance called out to him, "how about a time-out?"

Shadow shook his head. "No time for lollygagging, pup. We're going home."

"Wait. Shadow, I'm with you," Sassy said as she raced to keep up with her friend.

Chance jumped up on all fours and darted up the hill until he was side by side with Shadow. There was no way Chance was going to follow some cat—especially not Sassy—all the way home!

The three animals leaped over a guardrail and headed up an old service road to the interstate. The piercing, unfamiliar sounds of the free-way—speeding cars, blaring horns, and break-ing glass—made Chance, Shadow, and Sassy all the more homesick. After they had been travel-ing for quite a while, they reached the top of a hill. Shadow began wagging his tail furiously. "Hurry, we're almost home!" he shouted to the others.

Chance scurried happily to catch up with him. But when he reached the top of the hill, Chance's joy quickly faded to disappointment. He didn't see the Seavers' big gray suburban house or their fresh green lawn. All he saw was a bridge. And build-ings. Lots and lots of buildings.

"Funny. It doesn't look like home," Chance said.

"Over there. On the other side of that bridge, that's home," Shadow explained.

Sassy was disappointed. "But . . . but . . . it's so far away! And all those buildings . . . We'll never make it!"

"Of course we will," Shadow exclaimed. "Every step we take brings us that much closer to Peter."

Sassy knew that Shadow would travel forever to get back to his beloved boy. But she also knew that the old dog needed rest. So did she. "Shadow, stop," she said softly. "We're tired. We need rest."

Shadow looked back out toward the city. Home was very far away. "You're right," he agreed finally. "We should find a safe place to spend the night, and some food. . . ."

Bingo! Chance heard the magic word. FOOD! The hungry pup pointed his nose up in the air and sniffed. "Nose, don't fail me now," he said. He sniffed again, harder this time. His little tail wagged furiously. "What's this I smell? This is amazing! THIS SMELL IS A SMELL LIKE NO OTHER!"

Chance jumped happily into the air and shot off like a rocket in the direction of a nearby parking lot. There, in the middle of the lot, stood the object of his dreams—a Dumpster filled with leftover french fries, half-eaten hamburgers, and almost-empty milkshakes. Chance leaped up in the air and landed smack in the middle of a garbage buffet! "I'm in junk-food heaven!" he laughed.

After a while, Chance realized he was being self-ish. He'd been eating everything himself. Where were his manners? He should be sharing these riches. He sent a hamburger sailing out of the Dumpster. *Splat!* It landed at Sassy's feet.

Sassy sniffed at the meat and turned her head. "This is disgusting," she told Shadow.

"Help yourself," Chance called from inside the Dumpster. "There's plenty more where that came from."

"You'd better eat, Sassy," Shadow advised. "You'll need the energy for tomorrow."

Sassy bent down toward the hamburger, but she couldn't bring herself to taste it. "No. I can't do it. I'd rather starve than eat anything Chance considers food."

Shadow was growing impatient. It was time to find a place to rest. "Chance! That's enough. Get out of that thing!" he ordered.

"You kidding?" Chance answered between gulps. "A team of Saint Bernards couldn't pull me out of here!"

Just then, a huge garbage truck turned off the main street and into the parking lot where the Dumpster stood. Sassy leaped out of the way. Shadow hesitated for a split second.

"CHANCE!" the old dog shouted.

Chance had his head buried so far into the garbage he couldn't hear Shadow *or* the truck. The giant jaws of the truck lifted the Dumpster in the air and rocked it back and forth for a moment. Then the garbage—and Chance—landed with a thud in the truck's trash compactor.

"Man, oh, man!" Chance exclaimed. "That's one heck of a last call!" Suddenly he heard an ear-splitting whine, followed by a whirring sound. The truck driver had turned on the automatic trash compactor. The walls of the compactor were getting closer and closer. All around Chance, garbage was being crushed. It wouldn't be long before he was crushed, too!

With a cheeseburger still clenched between his jaws, Chance scrambled and clawed his way up to the top of the mountain of garbage. He reached the roof of the truck only seconds before the trash-compactor walls met! Chance jumped down from the truck and joined Sassy and Shadow.

Chance let out a big belch. "You know, I think I'm going to like it here," he told them.

Shadow and Sassy could not believe their ears. Didn't Chance realize what had almost happened? They stared angrily at him.

"What?" Chance asked innocently. "Did you want your burger with bacon?"

Chapter 6

At the very same time that Chance was chowing down, the Seavers were landing in Maine. As they got off the plane and entered the airport, Mr. Seaver heard his name over the public-address system. "Bob Seaver. Mr. Bob Seaver. Please report to the information desk."

Mr. Seaver dashed across the airport at top speed to the information desk. He could barely believe his ears when the airline agent told him that his animals had escaped. How was he going to explain this to the kids?

"There's been a problem," Mr. Seaver began

slowly when he returned to his family.

"Is it Shadow?" Peter asked nervously. "Dad, what happened?"

"They tell me the animals got loose somewhere . . . at the airport."

Mrs. Seaver looked out the window. It was pouring rain. "They're outside? In this weather!" she exclaimed.

Mr. Seaver took a deep breath and shook his head. "Not here. In San Francisco."

Peter and Hope were shocked. Hope began to cry. "How could we let this happen to them again?"

Mrs. Seaver wrapped her arm around her daughter's shoulders. "It was an accident, Hope. If the animals could survive a mountain wilderness, they can survive San Francisco, too."

"We have to go back!" Peter exclaimed.

Mr. Seaver shook his head. "There's no sense all of us ruining our vacation. I'll fly home first thing in the morning."

"No, Dad," Peter answered. "We have to stick together, good times or bad. We should *all* go back."

Jamie grinned. *They were going back—he'd be*

home to play in the next two baseball games.

Mrs. Seaver looked sternly at her son. "Jamie, you're not *happy* the animals are lost, are you?" she asked in disbelief.

"Mom, if we win these next two games, we make the play-off. The team needs me."

"Sweetheart, Chance could be in very serious trouble. He's your dog. *And* your very best friend."

Jamie felt a little guilty. He also still felt happy about the idea of playing in the big games. He was all mixed up. Tears welled in his eyes. He turned and ran away from his mother.

✳   ✳

Meanwhile, back in San Francisco, the animals were settling in for the night.

"This looks good," Shadow said, pointing to a corner in a trash-littered alley.

"But it's so filthy," Sassy whined.

"Good and filthy," Chance laughed. He was happy. Chance stood on his two hind legs and tipped over a garbage can. The putrid odor of rotten food filled the air. "You can't find decent trash like this in the burbs!" he exclaimed joyfully.

Shadow used his teeth to drag an empty card-

29

board box across the alley. "This ought to keep us warm and dry for the night," he said. Sassy crawled in and made herself as comfortable as possible. Shadow followed her.

Chance stood tall and stepped away from the box. "Uh-uh. Not for me," he said in his bravest tone. "I want to soak up this atmosphere."

Suddenly there came a crash. Then another. A tall, shadowy man wandered into the alley and lit a match right in Chance's face. That was a little *too much* atmosphere! The dog scrambled into the box.

"Well, look who's back," Sassy giggled. "And just when I thought it was safe to breathe again."

Chance tried to ignore her. He lay down, put his paws over his ears, and went to sleep.

All was peaceful—for a while. Then, suddenly, the animals awoke to a loud, metallic crashing sound. Chance looked up and stared into the face of a monster—a monster with huge glowing eyes and a mouth filled with broom bristles instead of teeth!

"Anybody know what this thing is?" Chance asked nervously. Shadow and Sassy were silent with fear. Cowering before what was actually a street-sweeping truck, the animals knew only that they had to escape its crunching metal jaws—fast.

The giant monster raced closer and closer. Any second now, it was certain to gobble them up!

Chapter 7

"RUN FOR YOUR LIVES!" Chance yelped as he dashed out of the cardboard box.

Sassy and Shadow wasted no time following him out into the alley. They turned around just in time to see the "metal monster" crush their cardboard box.

It took a little while, but Shadow finally found another place for the pets to rest—on a bench near a freeway underpass. Chance was exhausted. He was the first to fall asleep. It seemed as though he had slept only a few minutes (it was actually about three hours) when he felt Shadow nudge him.

"Rise and shine, campers. Time to go," Shadow ordered Chance and Sassy.

"What about breakfast?" Chance yawned.

Sassy stretched her long, lean legs. "Oh, my aching bones," she complained. "What I would do for a nice, soft, sleep pillow!"

Shadow was getting annoyed. "With any luck, you'll sleep on your pillow tonight—*if* we ever get moving."

But Chance and Sassy weren't ready to move. "Not so fast. Aren't we going to eat first?" Chance argued.

"And my morning bath. I don't do a thing until I've had my bath," Sassy added.

That was the last straw. Shadow looked them both in the eyes. "I'm going to count to three," he began, sounding like an angry parent, "and if you two don't shake a leg . . ." He left the punishment to their imaginations.

Sassy and Chance ignored his threats. After all, Shadow wouldn't hurt a flea (which, for a dog, was pretty incredible!). Shadow had to be bluffing.

But this was no bluff. Seeing that he was getting no reaction, Shadow reared up and pushed against the back of the bench with his two front paws. *Slam!* The bench toppled over, sending Sassy and Chance tumbling to the cement below.

Chance and Sassy stared up at Shadow in disbelief. "Who says you can't teach an old dog new tricks?" Shadow called back to them as he padded off in the direction of the main road.

✳   ✳

The animals traveled alongside the freeway for most of the morning. By noon they had reached the center of San Francisco. Although San Francisco was just a few miles from their home, it was as if these suburban pets had entered a whole new world. The city was teeming with people. The smells of spicy, delicious foods mixed with the scent of garbage. If the animals listened closely, they could hear the singing of street musicians almost being drowned out by the roars of buses, cars, trolleys, and trucks. And everywhere the animals looked, they saw buildings.

Chance was thrilled! This was just what he'd been hoping for—an exciting adventure! Sassy and Shadow, however, were a little less than enthusiastic. In fact, as the animals approached some abandoned buildings, Sassy grew downright scared!

"Which . . . which way, Shadow?" she stuttered.

Shadow stood for a minute and tried to sense which way to go. But he couldn't. "I'm not sure," he replied. "It's all so confusing."

Then, out of the corner of his *eye*, Shadow spotted a friendly face. A dog face! He trotted across the street to an abandoned gas station. A thin white dog sat on top of one of the old rusted cars.

"Hello, sir," Shadow greeted the dog.

"Hello," the white dog replied. "How goes it, brother?"

Just then, Sassy and Chance trotted up to Shadow. Before Shadow would answer the strange dog, he cautioned the others to be careful. The strange dog could be dangerous.

The white dog overheard Shadow's warning. "Dangerous?" he said with amusement. "Not me. I'm as friendly as a pat on the head . . . the name's Lucky."

"I'm Shadow. And this is Chance and Sassy. We're lost. We need to find the northern bridge that leads to the green hills."

Lucky shook his head. "Sorry. Never been there. Nobody has, 'cept for Riley. He might know the way."

"Do you know where we might find this Riley?"

Lucky's face grew fearful. "Can't tell you that, either. I like to keep my distance from him and his ilk," he whispered. "Wander around long enough, brother, and Riley will find you."

Shadow thanked Lucky and began trotting down the road in search of the bridge. Chance bounded up beside him. "Yo! Wait up," Chance said. "What's the hurry finding this bridge? We're here in the big city. Why not enjoy it?"

Shadow just sighed. The pup still didn't understand.

Chapter 8

"I can't go another step," Sassy whined.

Shadow slowed down, allowing Sassy to catch up. "Climb on my back and I'll carry you," the old dog said. Sassy leaped up and landed gently on Shadow's spine. She rested her paws on his thick, golden coat.

Chance couldn't believe his eyes. The dog he was supposed to look up to was carrying a cat? "Get a load of this," Chance griped. "Shadow, my friend, you are a disgrace to dogs everywhere!" Shadow grumbled a response, and the three animals continued down the street. Soon Sassy spotted a young boy sitting on the steps of his home with a kitten.

"Look, Shadow!" Sassy exclaimed. "Where there's a cat, there's cat food."

Not wanting to stop, Shadow scolded Sassy for not having eaten the night before.

"Eat that garbage Chance calls food?" Sassy said proudly. "Not in this life . . . or in the eight others I have coming."

Chance scoffed. He might eat garbage on occasion, but he was no fool. "What're you gonna do, fuzz-face? Hand the kid a can opener and an empty bowl? Get real."

"Watch carefully, canine, and learn," Sassy said coolly. She leaped off Shadow's back to approach the boy. The others watched in awe as she used her feline wiles, purring and prancing fetchingly until the boy leaned down to pet her.

That did it. Chance figured he was as good at getting food as anyone—especially Sassy—so he charged up the walkway and onto the porch with that very purpose in mind. Startled, the boy yelped and grabbed his kitten in fear. The front door opened with a bang. The boy's mother rushed down the stairs and pulled her son up the steps.

"Bad dog!" she shouted. "Go away!" The front door slammed behind them.

Dejected, Chance and Sassy turned to join Shadow on the sidewalk.

"Don't look at me," Sassy said to Chance. "I was on a roll . . . until you showed your ugly mug. You were a *bad dog*," she added for good measure.

Chance walked on ahead, confused. "Bad dog?" he said to himself.

Suddenly Shadow barked out a warning. "Chance!"

Chance whipped around in the direction of Shadow's voice. Whoa! Two angry-looking strays—a bullmastiff and a boxer—were practically right in front of him. The rough animals stood in the middle of the street, eyeing the three pets. Chance was the first one to speak. He said the first thing that popped into his head. "Bad dogs!" he scolded.

The strays didn't budge from their threatening stance—they were unimpressed. Retreating quickly, Chance turned silent. Shadow spoke up.

"We're looking for Riley. Can you help us?" he inquired.

Ashcan, the boxer, sniffed at Shadow and Sassy. Sassy arched her back and hissed. She did not like being sniffed. Ashcan turned his attention to Chance.

Chance wasn't too fond of being sniffed, either. "Yo! Down, boy," he snarled. "If I'd known we were going to sniff on the first date, I would've showered."

Ashcan did not appreciate Chance's sense of humor. "They're pets. Let's take 'em," he suggested to his buddy, Pete. Ashcan lunged for Shadow. He figured the old dog was the easiest victim.

Ashcan figured wrong. Shadow fought back—and hard! He nipped, bit, and kicked at the boxer.

While Ashcan kept Shadow occupied, Pete focused on Chance.

Chance was scared. Real scared. But he wasn't going to let Pete know that. Instead, Chance tried to do what he did best—talk his way out of trouble. "I feel obligated to warn you that I am a military-trained canine, expert in several disciplines of self-defense—"

Pete wasn't falling for that. He leaped at Chance.

"STOP!" Chance ordered.

Miraculously, Pete stopped.

"What's that long, furry thing growing out of your rear end?" Chance taunted. Pete twisted, turned, and stared . . . at his own tail!

"Made ya look!" Chance laughed. Then he chomped down hard on Pete's tail. Pete howled in pain. He tried to shake Chance loose. But Chance held tight to Pete's tail, dragging him down the street.

Sassy watched all the fighting with amazement. Suddenly Shadow called out to her. "Run, Sassy. Run!" he ordered.

The cat did as she was told. She dashed across the street and hopped onto a window ledge. From up there she could see all the way down the blocked street. Sassy gasped in terror. A huge pack of strays was bounding down the street. They were heading straight for Shadow!

Chance spotted the strays as well. "Shadow! They've got friends!" he cried out. Chance let go of Pete's tail and raced toward the pack. "I'll divert them!"

Chance ran straight toward the dogs at top speed. At the last minute, hoping they would follow him, he turned a corner, leaving Shadow in the clear. But the new group of dogs raced right past Chance and started to attack . . . Pete and Ashcan! Sassy breathed a sigh of relief. The newcomers were on their side!

The strays forced Pete up against the building, just beneath Sassy's perch. With a movement of her dainty paw, the cat pushed a clay flowerpot off the ledge. *Bam!* The pot landed right on Pete's head. Ashcan had seen enough. He backed off and ran away. Pete followed close behind.

Now that Pete and Ashcan were gone, a brown mutt, the leader of the pack, sidled up beside Shadow.

Oh no! Sassy thought. *What now?*

Chapter 9

Shadow sniffed at the brown dog. The brown dog sniffed back. Slowly the brown dog raised his tail and head, a sign of friendship.

"Our fight is with Ashcan and Pete," he said in a low, powerful voice. "Not you." The dog waited a beat and then introduced himself. "The name's Riley."

Shadow's mouth opened into a grin. "You're Riley! We've been looking for you. Sassy! Do you hear? It's Riley. He can show us the way home." Shadow looked around for Chance. Then he remembered. Chance had run off. "Chance," he said aloud.

"Who?" Riley asked.

"Our friend Chance," Shadow explained. "He thought you were with Ashcan. He tried to divert you from us. Where could he have gone?"

An old stray named Stokey stopped scratching his fleas long enough to point in the direction Chance had gone. Riley turned to a magnificent young dog. "Go, Delilah. Find their friend," he ordered.

Delilah took off down the street. Her strong legs moved so swiftly they seemed to blur. A love-struck mutt named Bando watched Delilah disappear down the alley and whimpered with longing. Another stray, named Sledge, saw Bando's pained reaction and turned to him, amused. "Get a grip, Bando," he said. "She'll be back in two wags of a tail."

The gang waited hopefully. If anyone could catch up with Chance, Delilah could.

✳   ✳

Chance turned off onto an abandoned street. He glanced behind him as he ran. Whew! The attackers were gone!

Chance slowed down to a mild trot. The young dog was very proud of himself. He'd faced danger and won. *What a rush!* he thought. *What excitement! What adventure!*

44

He turned around again. Delilah was racing toward him at full speed.

What . . . am . . . I . . . standing . . . around . . . for? Chance tore off, away from Delilah. Chance was sure she was the enemy. "Come on, feet!" Chance panted. He ran faster than he ever had.

Chance was fast, but Delilah was faster. She could run like the wind. It wouldn't be long before she caught up with Chance. Still, the sneaky young dog had one last trick up his paw.

Delilah ran until she reached the spot where she had last seen Chance. She looked around. Chance wasn't there. He'd disappeared.

"YAAAAAAAH!"

Delilah looked up toward the noise. She saw a howling black-and-white dog jump from on top of a truck. Chance landed on Delilah's back. A direct hit!

The two dogs wrestled, but Delilah quickly got the upper hand. She forced Chance to the ground, opened her jaws, and . . . licked him.

"You're cute." Delilah smiled. "Why did you jump me?"

What? This had to be a trick. "Don't play dumb with me, babe. I didn't just fall off the back of a

Jeep. Well, okay, so maybe I haven't exactly been around the block." Chance stopped for a second and thought about it. "Actually, I don't know a manhole from a pizza pie," Chance admitted. "But one thing I do know is this—*nobody hurts my friends.*"

Delilah shook her head. "Silly pup. We were trying to help you. I chased you to bring you back to your friends. Are you all right?"

Chance now looked at Delilah through new eyes. He sighed. "You are so beautiful," he answered.

Chance was in love.

Delilah and Chance walked in silence for a while. Chance could not believe his good fortune. Beautiful dog, beautiful day, and mounds and mounds of garbage to comb through. Chance trotted happily along, oblivious to everything but the gorgeous dog walking at his side. He didn't see the big red fire hydrant blocking his path only a few feet away. Suddenly, with an awkward bump, Chance found himself up against the hydrant. The startled and embarrassed pup quickly tried to regain his composure.

"How do you like living here?" he asked finally.

"It's okay," Delilah answered matter-of-factly.

Chance couldn't believe his ears. Okay? This was paradise! "But the sights! The sounds! The pervasive smell of garbage!" he exclaimed.

Delilah chuckled. "If you want, I'll show you around," she offered. Chance barked and wagged his stubby little tail. There was nothing he wanted more!

Delilah led Chance to her favorite part of the city—the park. Chance watched as a group of teenagers threw Frisbees back and forth across the lawn.

"This isn't what I wanted to see," Chance groaned. "There's too many trees, too much grass. It's too much like home."

"I think it's kind of pretty here," Delilah responded.

Chance snorted. "Believe me, pretty gets old fast. What I can't get enough of is good ol' shake, rattle, and boom."

Delilah laughed. Chance could be so cute and funny! She knew just the place to take him. But as Delilah turned to leave the park, a young man leaped out in front of her to catch a Frisbee.

"Watch out!" Delilah barked in warning to Chance.

Chance looked at the teen. He didn't seem too dangerous. "Him?" he asked Delilah.

She nodded. "Him or any other human."

Chance couldn't believe his ears. "Now, wait a minute," he said with amazement. "You're talking about the species that invented the chili cheeseburger."

But Delilah wasn't changing her mind. "Riley says humans can't be trusted, no matter how friendly they seem."

This was the first time Chance had heard anything like that. "But my humans treated me pretty nice," he insisted. "Gave me a home and everything."

Delilah sat back on her hind legs. Chance rested beside her. "When Riley was a puppy, he thought he'd found a home with humans, too," she began. Then she told Chance all about Riley's horrible puppyhood. About how Riley'd been all dressed up with a red ribbon and placed under a tree as a gift for a little boy. But when the boy saw Riley, he said he'd wanted a beagle. So the family dumped Riley on a street corner on the coldest, rainiest day of the year.

"Riley joined other dogs abandoned by humans.

48

Distrustful of all humans, they made a home of their own on the street," Delilah said sadly, finishing the story.

Chance had never heard anything so awful. The tale was really hard to believe.

"You mean I can't even trust Jamie?" Chance asked. "Jamie, who rescued me from the bad place? Probably saved my life?" Chance stopped and thought about that for a second. "But lately . . . ," Chance said with a frown.

"But lately," Delilah interrupted, "he's had better things to do than play with you."

"Maybe Jamie doesn't deserve my loyalty anymore," Chance admitted slowly. "Maybe *people* don't deserve our loyalty."

Delilah sighed. "That's what Riley says. I wouldn't know for sure. Never had a human family."

"What do you mean? All dogs have a home at one time or another."

Delilah rose to her feet. It was time to move on. "Not me," she whispered. "I was born a stray."

Chance looked over at Delilah with amazement. He'd never known a dog like her!

Delilah led Chance to a spot just near San Francisco's famous Fisherman's Wharf. The place was filled with yummy restaurants, street vendors, performers, and lots and lots of tourists. Delilah stood and watched the action from across the street. Riley had warned her never to go to Fisherman's Wharf. Too many people.

But Chance wouldn't let a little thing like Riley's advice come between him and all that food! He convinced Delilah to take a chance.

The dogs snuck up behind a hot dog vendor. Leaping in the air, Chance grabbed a frankfurter right from the man's hand. As the man turned to yell at Chance, Delilah swiped another hot dog and bounded off.

Chance and Delilah ran to the end of the pier, where a crowd had gathered to watch sea lions languish in the sun; the sea mammals rolled their large, fleshy bodies across wooden docks and every once in a while let out a territorial roar. Chance ventured slowly down the ramp that approached the strange animals. He hadn't got very far when, suddenly, one of the immense sea lions opened its jaws and let out a bark much fiercer than anything Chance could muster. Startled, the bulldog sprinted back up the pier to join Delilah.

Now that Chance was safe, he decided to have a little bit of fun. He barked back at the raucous animals and then rolled on his back, imitating the sea lions' agitated movements. Delilah laughed in delight and so did the crowd of people—they turned from the sea lions to take pictures of the barking, rolling dog.

Chance's next stop was the fish seller's stand. He watched eagerly as a crab escaped from its tank and scurried across the ground. Chance pounced on the unsuspecting crab . . . and got pinched right on the mouth. He howled in pain and embarrassment as he tried to free his lip from the crab's grip.

Not again! Chance thought miserably. This was the second time this had happened to him. The first time was when the three pets were lost in the wilderness, fishing for food. Boy, these little creepy-crawly things really had it in for him! Luckily, Delilah barked until the crab finally released its grip and crawled away.

Delilah gently nuzzled Chance's ear. She had never had such fun. Chance grinned. He thought he could really get used to city life.

51

Chapter 10

Meanwhile, Shadow and Sassy had almost given up on Delilah's bringing Chance back to them. They set off on their own to look for the pup. But it wasn't easy. Had the animals been back home in the suburbs, Shadow would have been able to figure out just where the pup was hiding. But the city was filled with smells, sounds, and sights that Shadow had never experienced.

"This place is so big, so crowded, yet I feel so alone. Sometimes I'm afraid I'll never see Peter again," Shadow admitted mournfully.

Sassy was shocked. Shadow had never given up before. "We count on you to be strong, to keep the faith, no matter what. So let's just keep mushing along," she urged her friend. "The sooner we find that doughnut-brain of a dog, the sooner we can go home."

Shadow sniffed at the air. Smoke! Flames! He turned the corner to discover the house they had visited earlier that day on fire! Shadow watched in horror as the same small boy raced back into the burning building to rescue his pet kitten. Without a shred of concern for himself, Shadow dashed after the boy and leaped in through an open window. Sassy followed close behind.

Riley and his pack of strays approached from the other side of the street. Riley couldn't believe his eyes. Shadow and Sassy were risking their lives for one of those *humans*!

Shadow crawled along the floor of the burning house. The brave golden retriever could barely see through the smoke and flames. Finally he spotted the boy. Gently, so as not to frighten him, Shadow crawled to the boy's feet and licked his hand. Then he quickly took the child's sleeve in his mouth and eased him toward an open window.

A large crowd of humans gathered around the burning building. They watched in amazement, then burst into applause, as the boy appeared in the window. Firefighters pulled the child to safety. No one noticed the old dog limping out of the house and across the street.

"I don't know why you'd do that for a human," Riley sneered as Shadow reached the pack of strays.

Shadow shook his head. "I'd do the same thing for a dog, a cat, or a mountain goat, Riley," the old dog explained. "All life is precious."

"Your friend showed a lot of guts goin' in there, too," one of the strays mentioned to Shadow.

Shadow's eyes grew wide. He'd no idea Sassy had followed him. "Sassy went in the house?" he cried out. He bounded across the street and toward the house. But a firefighter turned the hose on the old dog in an effort to keep him from the burning building.

Shadow didn't need to worry. Sassy knew just what to do. She made it through the flames and onto the windowsill. As soon as he spotted her, Shadow's expression changed from fear to pride. In her mouth Sassy held a tiny, mewing, frightened kitten. Sassy was a true hero. The brave Himalayan cat leaped down and deposited the kitten with her human. The boy scooped up his kitten and squeezed her tight. Then he lifted Sassy in his arms as well.

Sassy squirmed to free herself. "Easy does it, zippy," she meowed. "You're handling live merchandise here."

Shadow padded over to congratulate Sassy. But the boy's mother started to scream. "Jerry!" she called to her husband. "It's one of those horrible strays I was telling you about."

The little boy ran up beside Shadow. "That's the dog who saved me!" he explained to his mother. The little boy put Sassy down. Ever so slowly, the child reached out his hand and petted Shadow's thick golden coat. His mother's face softened as she watched her son. She owed a lot to the brave dog.

Sassy had an idea. "They'll take care of us," she whispered to Shadow.

Shadow shook his head angrily. "We have a home."

"Oh, all right." Sassy gave in. She scampered off after Shadow.

✳   ✳

After such a frightening experience, Shadow and Sassy needed to rest. They followed Riley back to the abandoned warehouse the strays called home.

"Hey, how about a little help finding that bridge?" Sassy asked Riley.

Riley shook his head. Going to the bridge was too dangerous. He wasn't going to take the risk just to help Shadow and Sassy find some *humans*.

Shadow wasn't ready to head for the bridge just then either. "Aren't you forgetting someone?" he asked Sassy.

Sassy pretended innocence. "Who?" she asked, a little too sweetly.

"Chance."

"Chance? Never heard of him," she retorted.

"You can't fool me, Sassy," Shadow chuckled. "You love the doughnut-brain as much as the rest of us. We're going to find that pup. And then WE'RE GOING HOME." He stated the last part very loudly, just to be sure Riley knew there had been no change in plans.

Riley led them into a large, dark, empty room in the abandoned warehouse. A few rays of light shone in through the high windows. What Shadow saw in the light left him angry . . . and relieved. There lay Delilah and Chance, resting comfortably.

"Hey, guys." Chance yawned. "What took ya so long?"

Sassy leaped angrily toward the young dog. It took two of the strays to hold her off. "Let me at him! I'll use him as a scratching pole," she spat.

"Chance! Where have you been?" Shadow demanded.

"With Delilah," Chance answered with pride, nuzzling his ladylove.

Shadow and Sassy weren't the only ones surprised by Chance and Delilah's romance. The strays were also pretty shocked. They let out a chorus of wolf whistles and then started in on Delilah. "Yo, Delilah," Stokey said tauntingly. "I didn't know you liked 'em young, dumb, and handsome."

Sledge chimed in. "Think you'll keep this one longer than two days, honey?"

The whole pack burst out laughing, except for Bando. He, of course, had thought Delilah would someday be *his* girlfriend.

"Delilah!" he pleaded. "You . . . I . . ." He could barely get the words out.

"Connect the dots, big guy," Chance taunted the shaken dog. "The suspense is killing me!"

That was all it took. Bando dashed forward, right at Chance. "She was going to be mine!" he snarled. Chance snarled back.

Riley let out a bark of warning. Bando went off to sulk in a corner. There was no doubt: in this pack of strays, Riley was boss.

Riley padded over toward Shadow. "I don't like this," he whispered, gesturing with his snout at Delilah and Chance. "It can only lead to trouble."

Shadow nodded in agreement. "I'll talk to them," the retriever said. He walked quietly across the room. Chance spotted him and yawned.

"Uh-oh," he whispered to Delilah. "Here comes that voice of reason. A genius of common sense. The master of all good . . . in a word, booorr-rinnnnng!"

Shadow thought for a moment. What he had to say was difficult. Still, it had to be said. "Chance, this thing between you and Delilah can't be . . . ," he began.

"Sorry, ol' feller. It already is," Chance interrupted.

"Don't you see? You're from different worlds," Shadow continued. "And Chance, you already have somebody to look after."

Delilah gave Shadow a distrustful look. "You

Chance breaks free from his carrier and sprints back toward the airport terminal.

In the main concourse of the airport, Shadow, Sassy, and Chance search for the Seavers, afraid their family will leave them behind *again*!

Sassy claws her way up the fence that borders the terminal, escaping the pursuing airport workers.

Tired and frightened, the three pets walk for miles in an attempt to find their way home.

Two streetwise strays, Ashcan and Pete, take a threatening stance as they size up the suburban pets. Little do they know that Chance, Shadow, and Sassy are not as tame as they seem.

Shadow arrives at the crest of a hill overlooking the strange, sprawling city of San Francisco.

Immediately enamored with the goofy Chance, Delilah gives him a tender caress.

Chance and Delilah decide to have a little fun at Fisherman's Wharf. Waiting until just the right moment, Chance snatches a hot dog right out of the counterman's hands!

Braving the smoke and flames, Shadow takes the young boy by the sleeve and guides him to safety.

The two dognappers slowly approach a preoccupied Chance. One prepares to entice the hungry dog with a cheeseburger, while the other lowers a noose.

Shadow, Riley, and the gang form a canine blockade in the street so Sassy can attempt to free Chance from the van.

The Seavers display some affection for their pets and the newest member of the family, Delilah.

Chance leaps acrobatically into the air in a vain attempt to grab the box of pizza.

Content at last, Chance wears some of the pizza and chomps away at the rest!

mean this Jamie character?" she asked. "He's a *human*." She spat out the word.

"We feel differently about people than Riley does, young lady," Shadow reprimanded her.

Delilah had heard enough. She rose on her four paws. "Come on, Chance," she said, staring right at Shadow. "Let's go someplace where we can be alone."

Chance looked from Shadow to Delilah. Which would it be? His old friend and teacher or his new love?

Chance stood up and trotted off after Delilah.

Chapter 11

Delilah led Chance to the roof of the warehouse. Together they looked out at the sun setting over the city. "You wanna stay here, Chance?" she asked quietly.

Had Chance heard what he thought he heard? He scratched at his ear in disbelief. "Come again?" he asked.

"Do you want to stay here in the city with me?"

Chance still couldn't believe it. "Come again?" he repeated.

Delilah was getting annoyed. "Stay. City. Me?" she snapped.

Whoopee! Chance was so excited he did a back flip. "Yes! Do I ever!" He jumped up and nuzzled Delilah playfully. She laughed and nipped at his ear. Chance leaped up, his tail wagging wildly with joy. Then, suddenly, Chance stopped and stood very still.

"What's wrong?" Delilah asked gently.

"It's Jamie," Chance said slowly. "He'll be alone if I stay with you."

Delilah sighed. *Not this again*, she thought. "He's a human, Chance. I'm a dog. Just like you."

That was true. Chance was confused. "But what about loyalty? What about all that man's-best-friend jazz?"

Delilah snorted. "Loyalty works both ways. You said Jamie didn't love you anymore. I guess it all boils down to who you trust more, Chance. Who do you love more? Me or him?"

Chance stared at the busy city below. He thought about Jamie and his baseball pals. Then he thought about the excitement of San Francisco and about Delilah. Chance knew what he had to do.

"I wanna stay here with you, Delilah," he answered quietly.

Delilah nuzzled him gently. "You know Riley and Shadow will try to keep us apart. Maybe we should run away. Then we can be together forever."

Chance nodded. "Let's do it! We can sneak away as soon as it gets dark!"

✳   ✳

Chance may have been convinced Jamie didn't care about him anymore, but Chance was wrong. For at the very moment that he and Delilah were planning their escape, Jamie and the Seavers were at the airport in Maine, waiting to fly home and find their pets.

"Mom, let's say I *was* worried about Chance," Jamie whispered to his mother, "do you think . . . do you think I'll *ever* see him again?"

Mrs. Seaver took a deep breath. "They found their way home once before, Jamie," she said confidently. "They can do it again."

Jamie smiled. Then he slowly drifted off to sleep, planning all sorts of fun things to do with Chance when he got home.

✳   ✳

It seemed everyone was making plans—Chance and Delilah, Jamie, even Shadow and Sassy. While

Sassy rested, Shadow and Riley climbed up to a nearby loading dock to discuss a good time for the pets to move on.

"The best time to leave is at night," Riley advised Shadow. "Fewer humans."

Shadow looked across the way. He spotted Delilah and Chance frolicking on the rooftop. The old dog's eyes grew moist. It seemed as though only two Seaver pets would be moving on tonight.

Riley understood Shadow's sorrow and tried to comfort him. "I know how you must feel, Shadow. It would be like losing Delilah. But I'll watch out for him. I'll watch out for both of them."

But Shadow would not be comforted. The streets were no place for Chance. And the only one who could convince the pup of that was Delilah.

Shadow watched as Chance and Delilah went back into the building. They walked out the front door a few minutes later. As soon as his paws hit the pavement, Chance started chasing the pigeons. The young dog never seemed to get tired of teasing those birds. With Chance distracted, Shadow went to speak to Delilah.

"Look at Chance, Delilah," the old dog said

gently. "He's not like you. He's not like any of the strays."

Delilah grinned. "That's why I like him," she replied.

"But he won't survive, Delilah. Not for long. The street will kill him."

Delilah wouldn't budge. "No! I'll protect him."

"But what if you can't? What if you become separated? What if something happens to him, Delilah? How will you feel?" Shadow stopped for a moment and let his argument sink in. Then he changed his tone and spoke softly. "You're the strong one, Delilah. You're strong enough to do it. And you will . . . if you truly love him."

Shadow moved on, leaving Delilah to watch her beloved Chance wrestle with a plastic tube of mustard. She loved him so. Delilah didn't know what to do.

Delilah's thoughts were interrupted as a blood-red van screeched around the corner. Delilah panicked. Riley had told her about the men in the blood-red van. They dognapped unsuspecting canines and took them to medical laboratories where humans tortured animals! Now these evil men were after Chance!

Two humans leaped out of the truck. One of the men pulled out a freshly cooked cheeseburger. The other pulled out a noose.

"Here you go, boy. You hungry?" urged the one with the burger.

Chance didn't know about the dangers of the blood-red van. He only knew his stomach was rumbling. Chance lunged for the burger. The man with the noose lunged for Chance! As one of the dognappers dragged the struggling Chance back to the van, the other one gave the pup a sinister smile and took a big, slow bite out of the cheeseburger. With his mouth full, he turned to his partner. "Throw him in back and let's get outta here."

Chapter 12

Delilah gave a loud, frantic warning bark. The strays stampeded from the warehouse.

"They've got Chance!" Sassy screeched as the blood-red van zoomed around the corner.

Delilah froze with fear. "It's all my fault!" she sobbed. "I was supposed to watch out for him."

"That doesn't matter now," Shadow responded. "We've got to stop them!"

Riley nodded. With a single bark he led the strays down a side alley. If they timed it well, the pack could still head the van off at the next street corner.

Riley was a seasoned general. And, as usual, his timing was perfect. Just as the van turned the corner, the strays poured out of the alley. The army of stray dogs taking a stand in the middle of the street surprised the men in the van, but it didn't scare them.

"I guess maybe they wanna dedicate their lives to science," snickered the dognapper driving the van.

His partner in the passenger seat responded with a sneering command. "Run 'em over. Stupid mutts." The driver obligingly stepped on the gas and sped toward the dogs. The strays scattered in different directions. Only Bando stayed by the truck. He leaped up in the air and flew through the window. The big mutt landed in the driver's lap with a thud! He growled menacingly.

The van screeched to a stop. The dognappers got out and ran, turning around only long enough to see Bando and the entire pack of growling, angry strays sprinting toward them. Unable to outrun the menacing dogs, the men began to yelp and howl in pain as each stray took a turn nipping and biting them.

While Bando and the others took their revenge

on the frightened drivers, Sassy leaped up on the rear bumper of the van. She came face-to-face with Chance. He was locked behind a metal gate.

Chance gulped. "Sassy!" he cried out with relief.

Sassy placed her paw on the metal screen. "Should I or shouldn't I?" she purred. She toyed with the lock. "Who is and shall forever be queen of the entire animal universe?" she jeered.

Chance sat back and whined.

"Say it!" Sassy insisted. She turned, as if to leave.

"You," Chance murmured.

Sassy put her ear to the wire door. "I can't heeeaaarrr you," she said.

Chance looked around him. Wherever this van was going, it was not a good place. "You! You're the queen of the animal universe!" he growled finally. "Now get me out of here!"

"Somehow I know I'm going to live to regret this," Sassy joked as she flipped open the latch. Chance leaped through the open door to freedom.

Riley, Shadow, Delilah, and Bando crowded around him. Chance laughed nervously. "Thanks, guys," he mumbled sheepishly. "Kind of a close one, huh?"

Delilah started to nuzzle Chance. But she stopped herself. The young stray looked at Shadow. Shadow returned her glance and slowly nodded. Delilah padded over to Bando.

"Bando, you're a hero!" she congratulated him. "You're hurt," she added, bending to lick his injured paw.

Chance watched the whole scene with horror. "Delilah?" he whimpered.

Delilah didn't look up. "I was wrong about you, Chance," she replied, doing her best to act as though she were speaking the truth. "You're not my type at all."

Chance was heartbroken. Delilah had dumped him for Bando, just as Jamie had dumped him for baseball. Nobody wanted him. The scared, lonely dog turned on his heels and dashed away.

"Chance! Stop!" Shadow called out to him.

"Just go, you stupid old dog," Chance howled back. "Go home without me." In a split second, Chance was gone.

Chapter 13

Chance wandered around the busy streets of San Francisco. He was alone in the crowds, but he was too upset to be frightened. He could smell the scent of delicious garbage coming from the restaurant Dumpsters, but he wasn't hungry. All Chance wanted to do was walk, walk, and keep on walking, until he reached the edge of the earth. Before long he'd traveled all the way back to the abandoned gas station where the pets had first met Lucky. Chance glanced over at a rusty old car. Sure enough, the skinny white dog was still sitting on its hood.

"Hello, Chance!" Lucky called out to him.

Chance stopped for a second and then moved on. He really didn't feel like talking.

"Don't be a snob," Lucky shouted out. "Come on over."

Reluctantly Chance padded slowly back toward the gas station. Lucky hopped down off the car and met Chance halfway.

"That's better," Lucky said gratefully. "I could use the company. Riley and his boys won't give me the time of day. In fact, they downright hate me. You see, I'm the enemy. I love my human."

His human? Chance looked around. The gas station was old and rusty. It looked as though there hadn't been a human there for a long time.

"Weren't you abandoned like Riley and the other strays?" Chance asked finally, trying his best not to insult the old dog.

Lucky stood proud. "No!" he answered, defending his owner. "Separated accidentally—like you. There's a world of difference between a dog that's been abandoned and one that's been lost. You and me, we're the lucky ones."

Chance snorted. Lucky? Not Chance. *Bad*-lucky maybe.

"We've got hope," Lucky explained. "I'm waiting for my human to come back and fetch me. Been waiting over six months now. I'll wait six years if I have to!"

Chance couldn't believe his ears. *Six months?* "But how can you be sure he'll come back? How can you be sure your human still loves you?"

Lucky gave Chance a long, hard look. "Friend," he said finally, "time can't change the bond between a man and his dog. Distance only makes it stronger." Lucky stared out over the horizon and nodded. "He'll come back for me. I just know it."

The old dog jumped back up on the car. Chance didn't know how Lucky could be so certain. Chance wasn't certain of anything anymore.

Chance wandered around the city until way into the night. Finally, when he felt his paws could carry him no farther, he stopped at the top of a steep hill. The city lights twinkled below him. San Francisco was so big, so full of danger. And somewhere out there, Delilah was with Bando. Could Chance ever win her back? Then again, what if Lucky was right? What if the strongest bond was between a dog and his human?

Chance needed time to think.

* *

Time was something Riley and the strays didn't have. Riley knew the blood-red van would soon be back—with more humans this time! The dogs had to move on quickly and make a new home. Riley began making plans. And those plans didn't necessarily include showing Shadow and Sassy the way to the bridge.

"Well, thanks for nothing," Sassy spat out.

"Sassy!" Shadow reprimanded her. He turned to Riley. "I'm sorry. You don't deserve that," he apologized.

But Riley shook his head. "No, she's right. I've been selfish," Riley admitted. "We come from two different worlds, Shadow. But that shouldn't keep you from rejoining your friends, even if they are humans. I'll lead you to the bridge. But we must leave soon. Now."

Shadow looked out down the road. There was no sign of Chance. Riley knew what the old dog was thinking.

"Chance made his decision," Riley told Shadow. "Now you have to make yours."

Shadow sighed. His heart was heavy. He would probably never see Chance again. Still, Peter needed him. "Okay," the retriever said sadly. "Let's go."

Riley turned and marched up the street. Sassy and Shadow trotted close behind.

It was a long, hard journey to the bridge. Along the way, the animals had to dodge trolley cars, trucks, windblown newspapers, and, of course, humans who meant them harm. Finally they reached the deserted street that would lead them to the bridge—and eventually to their home.

"Thank you, Riley," Shadow whispered, so as not to alert any humans. "You've been a good friend."

Riley wagged his tail. "We all walk on four legs, right?" he replied. The stray turned and trotted off into the night.

Shadow studied the bridge. But he couldn't seem to step toward it. After all, once he and Sassy went over the bridge, there would be no turning back; no possibility of seeing Chance ever again.

"I can't do it, Sassy," the old dog declared. "I won't. Chance needs me."

"But what about Peter? And Hope? They need us, too," Sassy urged.

"Believe me, I haven't forgotten Peter. But I'm not going to forget Chance, either."

Sassy backed up off the road. "Oh, I can't leave him behind any easier than you can," she admitted. Then she sensed something dangerous lurking in the darkness. She turned just in time to see Ashcan and Pete. They were back, and they wanted revenge for their earlier defeat. "Shadow!" she warned.

But it was too late. Ashcan and Pete were already snarling by Shadow's side.

"Where's your pal Riley *now*?" Ashcan taunted the old dog.

"Let us pass," Shadow said calmly. "We have no fight with you."

Ashcan and Pete leaped at the old dog. Shadow tried to battle them, but he was no match for the streetwise canines.

"HEY, PUMPKIN-HEADS! OVER HERE!"

A voice rang out from above. It was Chance! He stood on the hilly road that led straight up to the bridge. Ashcan and Pete focused their attention on the young dog.

"Why don't you dirtbags pick on someone your own age?" Chance dared them. "Nyah-nyah-nyah-nyah-nyah!"

That did it! Ashcan and Pete released their grip

on Shadow and raced in the direction of Chance's voice. Chance led them on a wild chase through a nearby construction site. "Watch out! Loose nails," he snarled. "Watch your step, boys. You're losing ground!"

Ashcan and Pete stopped for a second at the mouth of a wide pipe. They needed to catch their breath. Not Chance. He was full of energy! Chance dashed around to the other side of the pipe. "Hello!" he called.

Ashcan and Pete peered through the pipe.

"Looking for anyone in particular?" the brave dog laughed.

Ashcan and Pete were furious! They took the quickest route to Chance—right through the hollow pipe.

Chance couldn't believe how stupid those two dogs were! He quickly loosened the cement blocks that held the pipe in place. *Whee!* The pipe rolled down the hill, carrying Ashcan and Pete with it.

"Yeah! All right!" Chance cheered, dancing around in a victorious circle. "*Adios, muchos estúpidos!* Good-bye, idiots!"

But his joy was short-lived. As soon as the excitement of the battle was over and he knew

76

Shadow and Sassy were safe, thoughts of Jamie and Delilah once again filled Chance's mind.

Shadow and Sassy bounded up to Chance. "Are you okay?" Shadow asked.

"I'm hanging in there," Chance answered wearily.

"I never thought I'd hear myself say it, but . . . Chance . . . I missed you," Sassy admitted.

Had this been any other time, Chance would have really gotten on Sassy's case for that one. But Chance wasn't in the mood to tease Sassy. Even that didn't seem like fun to the heartbroken pup.

"How did you find us?" Sassy asked.

Chance shifted from paw to paw. "Actually, well, I've been following you since you left the warehouse," he admitted shyly.

Shadow let out a hearty laugh. "Well, pup, I'm glad you did," he said. Shadow looked down at the pipe. In the distance he could hear Ashcan and Pete still screaming for help. "We couldn't have made it without you!" he added gratefully.

"Well, rubber-face, I guess you're coming with us, after all," Sassy said.

Chance's face fell. "If Jamie still wants me," he replied quietly.

Shadow gave Chance a reassuring nudge. "He very much wants you, Chance, I can promise you that." Chance looked up at the older dog. He hoped Shadow was right, but he couldn't be sure.

Sassy began stepping toward the road. Shadow pulled up beside her. Chance lingered just one moment more. The young dog looked longingly toward the city. *Toward Delilah.* "She loved me. I just know it," he declared softly.

Shadow stopped for a second and waited for Chance to catch up. "A love not meant to be isn't any less real," he said cryptically. "What Delilah did was done out of love. One day you'll understand. Trust me."

Chance was confused. But this was no time to try and figure out another of Shadow's mysterious explanations. The pets had to get home.

"Shake a leg, canines," Sassy ordered. "I've got a hot date with my sleep pillow!"

Shadow, Sassy, and Chance ran up the access road onto the bridge. Wide-eyed, open-mouthed faces stared at the three animals through the windows of passing cars. The pets moved steadily with the traffic—they were determined to get to the other side.

Chapter 14

If Chance had had any idea what Delilah was really feeling, he would have felt much better. But Chance had no way of knowing that as he crossed over the bridge, back to life with the Seavers, Delilah was outside the warehouse, pleading with Riley to let her go with Chance.

"I've made a terrible mistake," Delilah sobbed. "I want to be with him. Forever."

Riley growled. "That's impossible! Even you must admit by now, the street is no place for a dog like Chance."

Delilah swallowed hard. She knew that her next

words would hurt Riley terribly. But they had to be said. "Maybe . . . maybe I could live in his world," she whispered.

Riley was shocked. "With humans?" he barked.

Delilah kicked at the ground. "They can't all be bad, Riley," she answered quietly.

But Riley had been hurt too badly by humans to ever forgive. He'd spent too many years on the streets to ever give a human a chance. "They *are* all bad, Delilah," he insisted. "Besides, what makes you think his humans will accept you into their home? A stray like you."

Delilah closed her eyes. Her ears flattened and her tail drooped. Riley's words cut into her like a knife. She let out a pained whimper. But Riley would not soften.

"I'm sorry, Delilah," he added sternly, "I don't want to hurt your feelings. But once a stray, always a stray." Riley turned and walked into the warehouse. This time, Delilah did not follow him.

✳   ✳

By the time the sun rose, Chance, Shadow, and Sassy had left the city far behind. They stood at the foot of the Golden Gate Bridge and stared out at the green, grassy suburbs of San Francisco.

"Home is just on the other side of those hills," Shadow said, using his snout to point in the right direction.

"Home. I can almost taste it," Sassy purred contentedly.

She followed Shadow across the road and up the hillside. Chance followed them halfway. Then, without thinking about his own safety, the heartbroken pup stopped in the middle of the road and turned again to look at the bridge.

Shadow and Sassy watched with concern. "Is he going to be all right, Shadow?" Sassy asked.

"Yes. Eventually." Shadow tried to convince Sassy as well as himself. He called over to the pup. "Come along, Chance. If we hurry, we'll be home for *supper*!"

But even the mention of food did nothing to cheer Chance. He just stood there, in the middle of the road. Suddenly Shadow's ears perked up. In the distance the old dog could hear the roar of a large tractor-trailer rig making its way over the bridge. The rumble of the engine swiftly grew closer and closer. That truck was moving fast!

"CHANCE!" the old dog warned. "Look OUT!"

Chance was so lost in thought that at first he didn't even hear Shadow's call. But as he slowly turned in the direction of his friend's voice, Chance came face-to-face with a huge, monstrous truck—coming *high speed* right at him!

For a split second, the dog and the driver of the truck stared into each other's eyes. Chance yelped. The driver screamed and slammed on the brakes. The huge truck swerved, then screeched to a halt.

A station wagon had been following the truck. The driver of the wagon slammed on *his* brakes, in a frantic attempt not to bash into the truck. The station wagon skidded off to the side of the road, barely missing the truck.

Shadow and Sassy watched in horror. When the smoke cleared, Chance was nowhere to be seen.

The station wagon rear door opened. Shadow's ears perked up as he heard a familiar voice cry out. "It's Shadow!" the voice said.

Shadow couldn't believe it. *Peter! It was Peter!*

As unbelievable as it may sound, it was the *Seavers'* station wagon that had been following the tractor trailer. Hope bounced across the back-seat and followed her big brother out the open door. "I saw Sassy!" she told her mother. "They're here! They made it!"

Sassy and Shadow bounded down the hillside and into their humans' loving arms.

Jamie stood alone at the side of the road. The boy looked in all directions for his pup. "Chance?" he called out. "Come here, boy." But the dog did not respond.

Mr. Seaver got out of the car and gently put his arm around Jamie. Then he turned and glanced at the stalled tractor trailer. Jamie followed his father's gaze. The boy's eyes filled with tears. Could Chance be dead?

Slowly Jamie bent down to look beneath the cab of the truck. His voice was shaky, but he called out once again to his dog.

"Chance, I love you. I really do," Jamie cried.

Jamie held his breath. At first there was no answer. Then, suddenly, a loud, happy bark came from beneath the truck. Out scampered Chance, untouched—except for a little grease on his fur.

Chance wagged his tail and jumped for joy as his boy hugged and kissed him. Then the pup finally heard the words he'd been longing for.

"Oh, Chance! I'm sorry I've been mean to you. I promise never to act like that again. Chance, *I love you!*"

No dog had ever felt so spectacular!

Chapter 15

It didn't take long for life to get back to normal at the Seavers'. Well, almost normal. Shadow went back to following Peter around. Sassy went back to lounging gracefully on her pillow. But Chance couldn't forget about Delilah. As much as he loved Jamie, and as happy as he was to know Jamie loved him, Chance had left a part of his heart in San Francisco. The pup didn't really get any joy out of chasing Sassy up trees anymore. He didn't get a thrill from burying remote controls, earrings, or shoes in the backyard. He didn't even really feel like begging scraps from the dinner table. Without Delilah, nothing seemed like fun.

Even though he couldn't know exactly what was wrong with Chance, Jamie knew his dog was sad. He tried everything he could to cheer him.

"Come on, Chance," Jamie called. "Let's play fetch!" The boy threw a ball out into the yard. Chance sat on the grass and looked up as the ball flew overhead. Then he sighed and rested his head on his paws.

Suddenly Chance jumped to attention. His ears perked up high on his head. In the distance, he could hear it. A familiar bark. A bark he had heard before.

It can't be, Chance thought. Then he heard it again. *But it sounds just like her. . . .*

Shadow and Sassy heard the bark, too. They came racing onto the porch, the Seavers following close behind. They watched as Chance tore across the yard.

Sure enough, there she was. "DELILAH!" Chance barked out joyfully. Chance went over and nuzzled her gently. Delilah nipped playfully at his ear. Chance and Delilah danced around, their tails wagging wildly.

"This is outrageous! This is amazing! Totally and

completely awesome!" Chance cried out with delight. "How did you find me?"

Delilah stopped playing. She nuzzled gently against Chance's fur. "I followed my nose, Chance . . . and my heart," she answered him.

Chance's heart skipped a beat. What if Delilah changed her mind about him again? He had to know. "For keeps this time? No going back?" he asked nervously.

"Yes. Forever and always."

Whoa! Chance couldn't believe how wonderful this all was. Delilah loved him. Jamie loved him! *Jamie!* Wait until Delilah met Jamie!

"Hey, Delilah, come here," Chance said, racing toward Jamie. "I want you to meet someone. . . ."

Delilah didn't move. All her life she'd heard how awful humans were. Still, if Chance loved this one, then maybe, just maybe . . .

Delilah crept slowly toward Jamie.

"Come on, Delilah," Chance coaxed. "He doesn't bite." Delilah sniffed at Jamie's outstretched hand. Jamie stroked Delilah's soft fur. Chance stood by and watched proudly.

"Can she stay, Dad?" Jamie asked his father.

Oops. That was something Chance hadn't considered. What if Mr. and Mrs. Seaver said no? Chance wasn't going to let that happen. Not after all he and Delilah had been through.

"Please . . . please . . . please . . . ," Chance yelped. "Ya gotta . . . ya gotta . . ." Mr. and Mrs. Seaver didn't understand Chance's words, but they got the message.

"I don't think Chance would have it any other way." Mrs. Seaver laughed. Chance watched nervously as she exchanged a glance with her husband.

"She can stay," Mr. Seaver agreed.

"Yes!" Chance yelped. He jumped up and did a back flip, landing right on his . . . rear! "I did that on purpose. Really," he lied.

Chance raised his nose in the air. A familiar smell wafted over him. Chance bounced to his feet. All right! It was time to introduce Delilah to one of the finer aspects of suburban life—pizza!

The pizza delivery man got out of the truck and tried making his way to the Seavers' door. Chance blocked his path. The delivery man tripped over Chance. The pizza box went flying in the air and landed right on Chance's head!

Chance was covered from head to toe in tomato sauce, cheese, mushrooms, and pepperoni. But he didn't care. He just took a big bite from a slice.

"Come on, family! There's plenty to go around!" he called out happily.